Put Beginning Readers on the Right Track with
ALL ABOARD READING™

The All Aboard Reading series is especially for beginning readers. Written by noted authors and illustrated in full color, these are books that children really and truly *want* to read—books to excite their imagination, tickle their funny bone, expand their interests, and support their feelings. With four different reading levels, All Aboard Reading lets you choose which books are most appropriate for your children and their growing abilities.

Picture Readers—for Ages 3 to 6
Picture Readers have super-simple texts, with many nouns appearing as rebus pictures. At the end of each book are 24 flash cards—on one side is the rebus picture; on the other side is the written-out word.

Level 1—for Preschool through First-Grade Children
Level 1 books have very few lines per page, very large type, easy words, lots of repetition, and pictures with visual "cues" to help children figure out the words on the page.

Level 2—for First-Grade to Third-Grade Children
Level 2 books are printed in slightly smaller type than Level 1 books. The stories are more complex, but there is still lots of repetition in the text, and many pictures. The sentences are quite simple and are broken up into short lines to make reading easier.

Level 3—for Second-Grade through Third-Grade Children
Level 3 books have considerably longer texts, harder words, and more complicated sentences.

All Aboard for happy reading!

T5-DHJ-670

To Kitty — G.H.

To my parents, Fred and Katie Heins — E.H.

Special thanks to Katherine Pradt.

Photo credits: cover, Andrew D. Bernstein/WNBA Photos; title page, p. 24 (right) Nathaniel S. Butler/WNBA Photos; p. 13, Andy Hayt/WNBA Photos; p. 14, Manny Millan/Sports Illustrated; p. 15, Rocky Widner/WNBA Photos; p. 16, John McDonough/Sports Illustrated; p. 17, Andrew D. Bernstein/WNBA Photos; p. 18, John McDonough/Sports Illustrated; p. 19, Barry Gossage/WNBA Photos; p. 20, (both) John McDonough/Sports Illustrated; p. 21, Louis Schaffner/WNBA Photos; p. 22, David Liam Kyle/Sports Illustrated; p. 23, Mike Wilkes/WNBA Photos; p. 24 (left) Bill Baptist/WNBA Photos; p. 25, Nathaniel S. Butler/WNBA Photos; p. 26, Bill Baptist/WNBA Photos.

Library of Congress Cataloging-in-Publication Data

Herman, Gail, 1959-
   WNBA, we got next! / by Gail Herman ; illustrated by Edward Heins.
      p. cm.—(All aboard reading. Level 3)
   Summary: Describes the formation of the Women's National Basketball Association, presents season recaps of the teams and player profiles, and gives an account of the first championship game.
   1. Women's National Basketball Association—Juvenile literature.
   2. Women basketball players—United States—Juvenile literature.
   [1. Women's National Basketball Association. 2. Women basketball players.] I. Heins, Edward, ill. II. Title. III. Series.
   GV885.515.W66H47 1998
   796.323'8—dc21   98-3087
                                                                            CIP
   ISBN 0-448-41866-5 (GB)   A B C D E F G H I J   AC
   ISBN 0-448-41865-7 (pbk.) A B C D E F G H I J

ALL
ABOARD
READING™

Level 3
Grades 2-3

WNBA
We Got Next!

By Gail Herman
Illustrated by Edward Heins

With photographs

Grosset & Dunlap • New York

The First Game

It is June 20, 1997. Inside the Great Western Forum in Los Angeles, sports history is about to be made.

The lights go down. The crowd is quiet. The voice of the announcer booms, "Ladies and gentlemen! The WNBA!" And onto the court come the Los Angeles Sparks and the New York Liberty.

It is the first game of the Women's National Basketball Association. It is also the first pro women's basketball game ever to be on network TV.

The fans are so excited—little girls, most of all. They leap to their feet. They hold up signs. The signs say, "We Got Next!" That means, we get the court next. It's our turn.

And for the WNBA, indeed, it is.

The Beginning

Girls started playing basketball in 1892, less than a year after the game was invented. The rules in girls' basketball were different. Only one girl on each team could play full court. A player had to pass or shoot after three dribbles. This slowed down the game a lot.

It took a long time for the rules to change. But girls' basketball slowly became a faster, more exciting game.

Then, in the 1970s, a law was passed. It said that schools had to treat girls'

teams the same as boys' teams. This meant more money for better coaches and better equipment for girls' teams. What was the result? Better players, of course.

You could certainly see that in women's basketball. In the 1976 Olympics, the U.S. women's team won the silver medal. That was the very first time women's basketball was played in the Olympics. The U.S. women's team then picked up gold medals in both the 1984 and 1988 games.

In 1995 the talented University of Connecticut women's basketball team started making headlines. They played an undefeated season. Led by six-foot-four Rebecca Lobo, they aced the college championship, too.

Then came the 1996 Olympics. The U.S. team had Rebecca Lobo and other college basketball stars like Sheryl Swoopes and Lisa Leslie. These women were unbeatable. Unstoppable. They won the gold medal. The players appeared on TV talk shows and magazine covers. Suddenly lots of people were hooked on women's basketball.

The NBA took notice. People had tried to start women's pro leagues in the past. But they never lasted. One folded after just one game! But now was the time for pro women's basketball to be played in NBA arenas and shown on TV. Just the same as the guys.

The pressure was on.

The 1997 Season

In just a little more than a year, the league was formed. It had two conferences with four teams each.

How did the season play out for the WNBA? It was an exciting one—full of thrilling wins, crushing losses, and hold-your-breath buzzer-beating shots.

Here's a team-by-team look at the highlights and the star players of the very first season:

Western Conference

Utah Starzz, 4th place

Record: 7 wins, 21 losses

Player profile: Wendy Palmer (center) led her University of Virginia team to championship titles. She was second in rebounds for the WNBA.

Season recap: The Utah Starzz were the only team that were never in line for the playoffs. Even with many good players, they were outscored an average of 10 points a game. Still, they pulled off some great upset victories—like their win against the mighty Houston Comets.

Sacramento Monarchs, 3rd place

Record: 10 wins, 18 losses

Player profile: Ruthie Bolton-Holifield (guard) had been the leader of the 1996 Olympic team. In college, coaches told her she'd never be a star player. But she sure proved them wrong.

<u>Season recap</u>: Early on, the Sacramento Monarchs seemed headed for greatness. Ruthie Bolton-Holifield had a "double-double" in the first two games. That means she scored in the double digits and had rebounds in the double digits, too. But then both Ruthie and Chantel Tremitiere, another star player, hurt their knees. And the team just couldn't get back in sync.

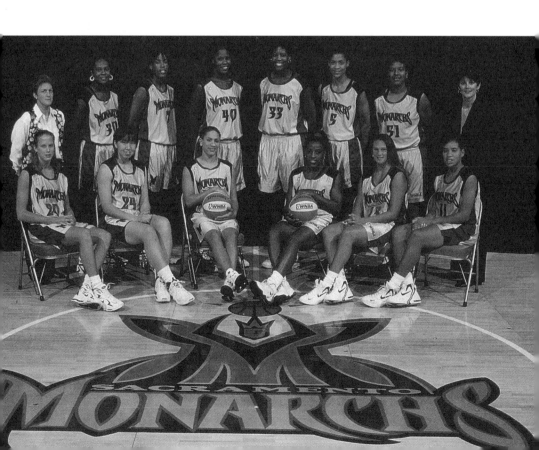

Los Angeles Sparks, 2nd place

Record: 14 wins, 14 losses

Player profile: By the time Lisa Leslie (center) was in the seventh grade, she was six feet tall. Back then, she played on an all-boys team and ended up being the team MVP! Lisa was first in the WNBA for rebounds.

Season recap: From the beginning, the
L.A. Sparks were favored to win the
WNBA championship. But they lost
their first two games. By midseason,
L.A. had twice as many losses as wins.
So the Sparks got a new coach. Right
away they started to play better. They
even beat the top-ranked New York
team 67–50. But they missed a playoff
spot by only one game.

Phoenix Mercury, 1st place

Record: 16 wins, 12 losses

<u>Player profile</u>: Michele "Tank Girl" Timms (guard), from Australia, was the team leader and the team joker. She loved the fans and would stay for hours after a game to sign autographs. Once she even wrote a letter to a newspaper saying she was sorry she had had to leave so soon!

Season recap: This team was strong from the beginning. Phoenix had a run of six wins in seven games. Then the streak turned sour—six losses in a row! During the last game of the season, they played the tough Los Angeles Sparks. Back and forth, they traded leads. At the end of the game, the score was tied. It was 64 to 64. That meant overtime. But by the final buzzer, the Phoenix Mercury were in the playoffs!

Eastern Conference

Charlotte Sting, tied for 3rd place
Record: 15 wins, 13 losses

Player profiles: Andrea Stinson (guard)
and Rhonda Mapp (center) had been
friends since high school, when they
played in summer leagues together. They
even went to the same college—North
Carolina State.

Andrea Stinson

Rhonda Mapp

Season recap: The Sting had a rough start. But they ended up in a playoff spot, thanks to Andrea Stinson. She scored 29 points in one game—and that was while she had a stomach virus!

Cleveland Rockers, tied for 3rd place

Record: 15 wins, 13 losses

<u>Player profile</u>: Lynette Woodard (guard) was the first female player on the Harlem Globetrotters. The Globetrotters were a show team. All over the country, they made people laugh with their tricky passing and shooting. Lynette also led the U.S. women's Olympic team to the gold in 1984.

Season recap: The season was a roller-coaster ride for the Rockers. After only three games, star guard Michelle Edwards hurt her knee. She missed eight games. By the time she returned, the team had a terrible record. They did rally, but they lost the last regular-season game to the New York Liberty. This dashed their hopes for the playoffs.

New York Liberty, 2nd place

Record: 17 wins, 11 losses

Player profiles: Rebecca Lobo (forward-center) was a 1996 Olympic winner and one of the league's biggest stars. Teresa "Spoon" Weatherspoon (guard), the heart and soul of the team, was named Defensive Player of the Year.

Teresa Weatherspoon

Rebecca Lobo

Season recap: The New York Liberty were the team to beat. They started off with seven straight wins. But then they began to stumble. Near the end of the season, they had four losses in a row. Would the Liberty make it to the semifinals? It all came down to one game against the Cleveland Rockers. With forty seconds left in the game, the score was tied, 69-all. Then, in overtime, New York won the game. On to Phoenix and the semifinals!

Houston Comets, 1st place

Record: 18 wins, 10 losses

Player profile: Cynthia "Coop" Cooper (guard) barely touched a basketball before she turned sixteen. She was voted MVP of the entire league.

Season recap: No one expected much from the Comets with their star player, Sheryl Swoopes, out of the picture. (She had a baby just four days after the season began.) But Cynthia Cooper stepped in as team leader. In one game she scored 30 points. Then 32. In her best game she scored 44 points—12 in a row! By August 12, Houston had the best record in the league. The Comets knew they'd be going on to the semifinals.

By August 24, 1997, eight teams were cut to four:

New York vs. Phoenix.

Houston vs. Charlotte.

Which teams were going to take the titles? Which one would grab the championship game?

The Playoffs

New York felt strong going up against the Phoenix Mercury. And they were. They took an early lead and they never let up. By the final buzzer, it was New York 59, Phoenix 41. The Liberty kept Phoenix to the lowest score in league history to date.

The New York Liberty were headed to the championship.

The Houston Comets faced the Charlotte Sting. The first half was close. Charlotte was up by only 4 points.

But Houston fought back in the second half to tie the score at 48.

Then disaster struck.

Houston Comet Wanda Guyton and her teammate Tina Thompson both went for a rebound. They smacked right into each other. And Wanda was knocked out cold.

The game stopped. Doctors rushed over. Wanda had to be taken by ambulance to a nearby hospital.

The Houston players were shaken. But they didn't let the accident stop them. Cynthia Cooper scored point after point— 31 in all. Houston beat Charlotte 70–54. It was the best medicine for Wanda Guyton, who, luckily, had only a neck sprain and a mild concussion.

So it was New York against Houston. Teresa Weatherspoon and Cynthia Cooper had won the gold medal together on the 1988 Olympic team. Now Spoon and Coop were to go head-to-head in the first WNBA championship game in history.

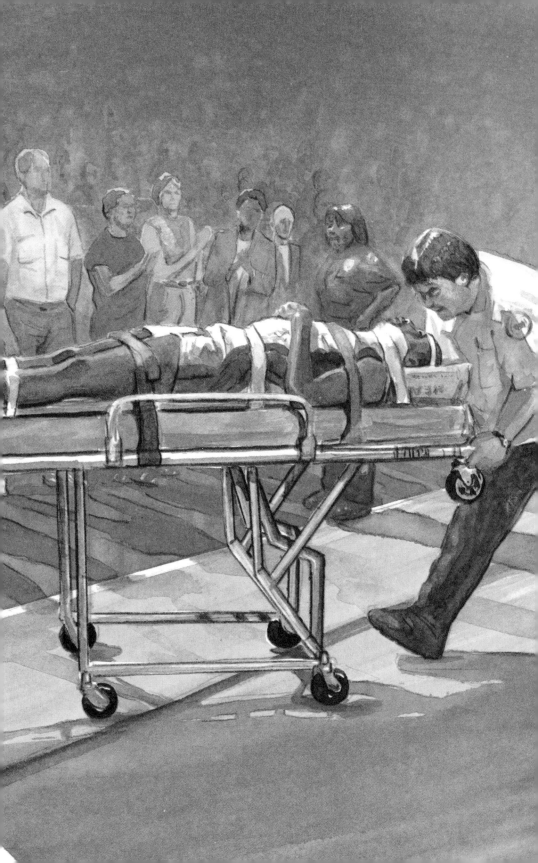

The Championship

Houston, August 30, 1997. The WNBA championship game.

An excited crowd fills the Summit. Cynthia Cooper's mom, Mary Cobbs, is there. She wears a T-shirt with a photo of her daughter on it.

Mary Cobbs has breast cancer. She's had weekly treatments since April, and Cynthia has been by her side every time. The Comets coach even changed practice times so Cynthia could be with her mom. And in return, her mother hasn't missed a single home game.

Despite all her worry about her mom,
Cynthia is always the first player out on
the court. She's been training harder
than ever. She's become a real hero to
her teammates—and to the fans.

People say this is what makes the

WNBA so great. The human side of it. Players really connect with the fans. Players give their time—in basketball clinics and at autograph signings after the games. They want to encourage young girls to play sports, to be the best they can.

Now the biggest game of the season is about to begin. Houston fans hold up signs. They say "Take It to the Hoop, Coop." Even before the players appear, the crowd is on its feet. Wanda Guyton cheers, too. She still can't play, and watches from a wheelchair.

Then it's the tipoff. Tammy Jackson and Kym Hampton face each other. They jump. Houston has the ball. But not for long.

Everyone plays hard. By halftime, Cynthia has scored 11 points. Houston holds a slim 28–24 lead.

Then, two minutes into the second half, Kym Hampton drives in a layup. The Liberty are only 2 points behind.

This could be it. A comeback for New York.

The Comets answer back by scoring 10 points in a row. Three minutes later, Rebecca Lobo makes a basket to end the Comets' streak. But then Cynthia Cooper makes eight straight free throws. After that, the New York Liberty never get back in the game. The final score is 65–51. For Houston.

42

Lights flash. Streamers rain down on the court. Cynthia runs into the stands to her mom. Players hug one another. Wanda Guyton is wheeled out, and the team is together. The Houston Comets have won the very first WNBA championship ever!

What's Next?

So, what's next for the WNBA? Now there are teams in Detroit and Washington, D.C. There is a longer playing season, too.

In the first season alone, more than a million fans came out to see the WNBA. About one-third were kids and teenagers. Many had never even been to a pro basketball game before.

More and more young girls go to
games with their families. Or they go on
trips with their school teams. Or for a

friend's birthday party. They wear jerseys with their favorite players' names on them. They watch, and dream.

"When I saw a WNBA game, it made me think maybe I could play basketball like that, too," said a nine-year-old fan.

In this next season, the WNBA has next—again. And in seasons to come? Who knows who will step in to continue.

Maybe *you*.

WNBA
We Got Next!

By Gail Herman • Illustrated by Edward Heins

This book belongs to

_____

(your name)

I have read it all by myself!